Nighttime
at the ZOO

Written By Dale Smith
Illustrated By Gwen Clifford

Golden
Anchor
Press
Tacoma, Washington

THIS BOOK IS DEDICATED--

To *Ethel Skipworth Rhoads Smith.* Mother, you lovingly sang "The Zoo Lullaby" to your children, grandchildren, and great-grandchildren. Through this book countless others will share it with little ones they love. Thank you! --D.S.

To *Lem and Jean Rogers*, my artistic and loving parents, who gave their everything for so many years and who continue to smile on me and my love of art.--G.C.

Publisher's Cataloging in Publication
(Prepared by Quality Press)

Smith, Dale, 1932-
Nighttime at the zoo/ written by Dale Smith ; illustrated by Gwen Clifford.
p. cm. -- (Grandad, tell us a story)
SUMMARY: A storytelling grandfather gets two children ready for bed with a story-song about children visiting a zoo at dusk.
ISBN: 1-886864-10-1

1. Zoo--Juvenile fiction. I. Clifford, Gwen, ill. II. Title.

PZ7.S657Ni 1997 [E]
QBI96-20391

Library of Congress Number 96-094349

Published by Golden Anchor Press
1801 S. 112th St., Tacoma, WA 98444
Printed in Hong Kong by C&C Offset Printing

This book is printed on acid free paper.
(So your children can pass it on to their children.)

First Edition
9 8 7 6 5 4 3 2 1

Cover Design by Lightbourne Images, Ashland, OR

"There he is, Tracie, there's Grandad!" said Ricky to his sister, as they peeked into the den.

Ricky and Tracie were visiting Grandmother and Grandad Smith at their farm in the hills of Kentucky.

It was almost bedtime. That meant it was time for a bedtime story!

"Grandad, tell us a story," said Tracie.

"O.K.," agreed Grandad. "You two climb right up here with me."

"Tell us about when you were a little boy, Grandad," said Ricky.

"Hmmm, let's see....When I was little, there were no TVs. Our family didn't even have a radio. But we had something better! Better than radio, even better than television. Do you know what it was?"

"Uh-uh, I don't know," said Ricky.

"I don't either," said his sister. "What was better than television, Grandad?"

"Story time...we had story time! It was especially fun in the winter. We'd sit around the fireplace, eat popcorn and tell tales. My mother had a super-special story I liked better than any of the rest."

"Tell us that one!" begged the children.

“Well....maybe. It was about a family that lived across from the zoo. The children in the family loved to go to the zoo when it was just getting dark. It was such fun to watch the sleepy animals getting ready for the night.

"The story was in the form of a song," continued Grandad, "a very special song called 'Nighttime at the Zoo.' I loved to hear my mother sing it.

"Sometimes, when she tucked me in at night, she'd sit on the side of my bed and sing it just for me."

"Sing it for us, Grandad," said Tracie.

"No, I'd better not do that," said Grandad, with a twinkle in his eye. "It's a magic song! The magic is that it'll make you sleepy."

“C’mon, Grandad,” said Ricky, “you’re teasing us! We won’t get sleepy! Please sing it.”

“Well, O.K. Since it’s bedtime, it wouldn’t hurt for you to get a little sleepy. As I sing, you imagine you’re the children visiting the sleepy animals. Here goes... Ummmmmp, Ummmmmmp!” he cleared his throat, then he began to sing.

ZOO
When the shades of night are soft - ly creep- ing, Down a - cross the gar - den at the zoo,
Chil - dren would you like to take a peek in

At the sleep - y lions and kan - ga - roos?

Ros - a - lie the po - lar bear is slum - b'ring,

Hear the par - rots talk - ing in their sleep.

And the mon - keys off their perch - es tum - bling,

One by one lie hud - dled in a heap.

Good night, Mis - ter E - le - phant.

Ti - gers, cease your play!

Lie down, and you're sure to dream

That you're roam - ing in the jun - gle far a - way.

Sleep well, Miss - us 'Rang - u - tan,

Good night, ze - bras too.

When an - oth - er day is break - ing, You will all of you be wak - ing,

ZOO
SNAKES

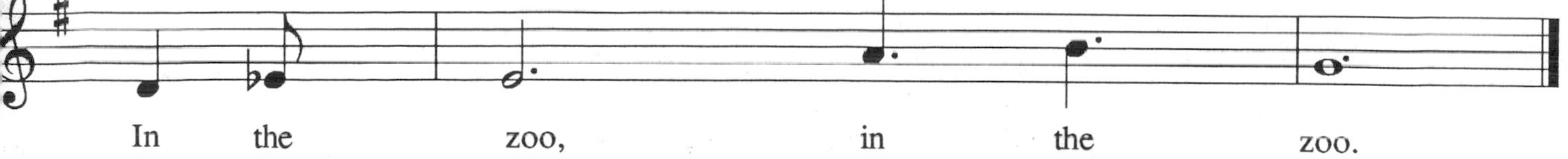
In the zoo, in the zoo.

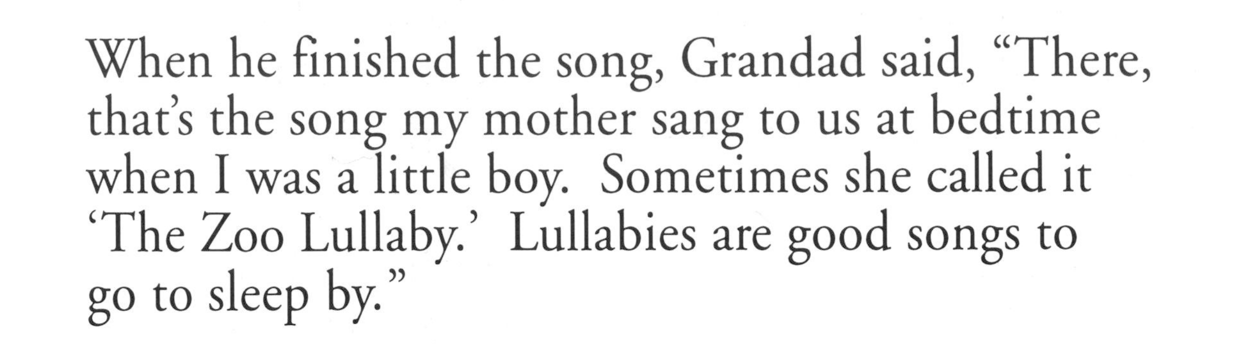

When he finished the song, Grandad said, “There, that’s the song my mother sang to us at bedtime when I was a little boy. Sometimes she called it ‘The Zoo Lullaby.’ Lullabies are good songs to go to sleep by.”

"Shhhhhh...Look, Grandad," said Ricky, "Tracie's already asleep. Please sing the song one more time so I can learn it. Then when I get big I'll sing it to my children."

So Grandad gently sang the song again. When he finished, he asked softly, "Children, did you like that?"

All they said was, "Zzzzzzzzz, Zzzzzzz." The song had worked its magic. They were sound asleep and dreaming pleasant dreams. In her dream, Tracie was roaming in the jungle far away. And Ricky dreamed of being grown and singing "The Zoo Lullaby" to his little children.

Grandad picked up the grandchildren and softly hummed the song once more as he carried them upstairs and tucked them in.

The End

A LETTER FROM THE AUTHOR

Dear Friend of Children,

Story time! This book is about story time. It's about big people and little people connecting through story telling. What a tool stories are to enrich the lives of children! Fairy tales and old classics are great. Learn several of them well so you can tell them with confidence and enthusiasm. Then turn your creativity loose and develop your own stories with imaginary places, people and animals. Kids will love them!

Children especially like two types of stories. You'll frequently hear, "Tell about when *I* was *little."* Kids want to hear repeatedly about how special they were. About how excited you were when they were born. About how brave they were when they had to have a shot--or similar episodes from their young lives.

The second often-requested story type is "Tell about when *you* were *little."* Such stories provide opportunity to help children connect with their extended family and ancestry. Tell of your victories. They will thrill to your story of the big fish you caught, and about when your shot won the basketball tournament, or when your cake took first prize. But they also need to know about when you fell through the ice and almost drowned. Or about how you tried out for cheerleader three straight years and didn't make it. Your victories will help them anticipate their own achievements. But the fact that you failed at times, and yet are "the wonderful you" they love so much, will help them face their failures with optimism.

The child will want to hear some stories over and over. Some may become family traditions. The story-song that is the basis of this book is a tradition in our family. My mother sang it to my sister and brother, Rhea and Reg, and to me, from our earliest memories. Now, five generations have enjoyed it. I hope it will become a part of your family heritage, too. Little children love it--this I know! Perhaps you can sing it from the music score accompanying the story. Or you may get a tape of the book, if you haven't already done so. If your bookstore doesn't have it, you may send $5.95 plus $2. shipping/handling to Golden Anchor Press, P.O. Box 45208, Tacoma, WA 98445-0208. By the way, kids don't care whether you sing it well, or not. Just sing it to them! As one child said, "We're mostly here for the cuddling!"

As I conduct "Every Kid A Winner!" seminars across the nation, families tell me about enriching experiences they have with story time. What great tales I hear! I'd be happy to have you send me yours. Keep adding to your repertoire of stories--and continue to build a tradition of story telling with your family and with other children. It's a wonderful way we can work to make "every kid a winner."

Best wishes,

Dale Smith

Dale Smith

P.S. After your children have read the book several times, point out that pictures of the grandfather and children include a little mouse. And each zoo picture has a secondary "critter," such as a cat, butterfly, bird, caterpillar, peacock, turtle, etc. Looking for these will strengthen the child's skills of observation and add to their enjoyment of the book. Happy story-sharing!

Nighttime at the Zoo